Eneèko Nàmbe Įk'ǫ̀ǫ̀ K'eèzhǫ

The Old Man with the Otter Medicine

1993 **John Blondın** *nįhtł'è yį̀tł'è*
(Wetà **George Blondın** *wegondı)*

Told by **John Blondin** *in 1993*
(as told by father, George Blondin)

Illustrated by Archie Beaverho
Translated by Mary Rose Sundberg

Theytus Books

Library and Archives Canada Cataloguing in Publication

Blondin, John, 1960-1996.
Eneèko nàmbe ik'oò keèzho / 1993 John Blondin nihtłè yìitłè;
wetà George Blondin wegondi = The old man with the otter medicine / told
by John Blondin in 1993 ; as told by father, George Blondin ; illustrated
by Archie Beaverho ; translated by Mary Rose Sundberg.

Accompanied by CD-ROM in jewel case.
Includes bibliographical references.
Text in Dogrib and English.
ISBN 978-1-894778-49-7 (bound).--ISBN 978-1-894778-69-5 (pbk)

1. Dogrib Indians--Folklore. 2. Dogrib language--Readers.
3. Fishers--Folklore. 4. Otters--Folklore. 5. Oral tradition--Northwest
Territories. 1. Dogrib (Indiens)--Folklore. 2. Dogrib (Langue)--
Lectures et morceaux choisis. 3. Pêcheurs--Folklore. 4. Loutres--
Folklore. 5. Tradition orale--Territoires du Nord-Ouest.
I. Beaverho, Archie II. Blondin, George, 1923- III. Sundberg, Mary
Rose IV. Title. V. Title: Old man with the otter medicine.

E99.T4B563 2007   398.2089'972   C2007-901730-4
E99*

Printed in Canada

Published by Theytus Books
Advising and Proofing by Anita Large
Design by Suzanne Bates
Copyediting by Julie Turner
www.theytusbooks.ca

Multimedia CD by www.bogglenoggin.com

On behalf of Theytus Books, we would like to acknowledge the support of the following:
We acknowledge the financial support of the Government of Canada through the Book
Publishing Industry Development Program (BPIDP) for our publishing activities.
We acknowledge the support of the Canada Council for the Arts which last year invested
$20.1 million in writing and publishing throughout Canada.
Nous remercions de son soutien le Conseil des Arts du Canada, qui a investi 20,1
millions de dollars l'an dernier dans les lettres et l'édition à travers le Canada.
We acknowledge the support of the Province of British Columbia through the British
Columbia Arts Council.

Acknowledgements:

Storytelling has been part of Dene life for centuries. Although John is being acknowledged as the author of these legends, the stories come from several generations of Dene oral tradition. These stories originate from the Sahtu Region of the Northwest Territories. As he grew up, John's parents George and Julie Blondin maintained the storytelling tradition of passing along the ancient teachings to their children. John, a gifted storyteller in his own right, presented and performed some of these stories publicly to educate children. Barb Cameron, then curator of the Prince of Wales Northern Heritage Centre recorded John's words. Today, John's father, George Blondin, a well-known and respected Elder continues to write and share the Dene teachings.

This particular project came to be out of a need for more literature portraying the Dene culture and languages both in the classroom and on the public bookshelves. We presented this story again at an Aboriginal Illustrators Workshop where Archie Beaverho brought it to life again with his painting. Mary Rose Sundberg translated it into Dogrib and through a joint project with the Yellowknife Catholic Schools, Yellowknife District Education #1 and through Theytus Books they have been published for your enjoyment. The entire project was coordinated by Dianne Lafferty, Aboriginal Language & Culture Coordinator for Yellowknife Catholic Schools.

In written form, these legends about medicine power, and a time almost forgotten, will now be passed along to anyone who chooses to read them. More importantly, they may be shared with Dene people, especially their children who will follow them into the future.

George Blondin - Storyteller
John Blondin - Storyteller
Archie Beaverho - Illustrator
Mary Rose Sundberg - Translator and Dogrib Narration
Dianne Lafferty - English Narration

*This publication was partially funded by the Government
of the Northwest Territories and the Government of Canada
through the Department of Canadian Heritage.*

BRITISH COLUMBIA ARTS COUNCIL
Supported by the Province of British Columbia

Canada Council for the Arts   Conseil des Arts du Canada

Canadian Heritage   Patrimoine canadien

Northwest Territories Education, Culture and Employment

Yellowknife Catholic Schools

When I was a young man, before TV and everything young people have today, our only source of entertainment was to sit around campfires and listen to our grandparents tell stories. During the day, we all worked hard in order to survive and listened to stories in the evening. We did not go trapping and hunting on weekends, we did this for the whole year. This is how we lived. This is how we survived till today. The modern way we live today is totally different.

My grandparents told me many stories that I was supposed to transfer to my children and as many people as possible. Many of my stories are a history of my people and our culture. I have told many stories in my travels but people today are very distracted by everyday business. My fear was that our stories would be lost in the future. The only way to preserve our stories is to put it in writing so people and school children can read them when they want in the future.

I dedicate this book to the future of the Dene and encourage everyone to read these stories to better understand our culture and visualize how hard life were for the Dene in the past. Remember these stories and tell them to other children. I thank you all for the interest you have shown and doing this for me.

Masi Cho
George Blondin

The Dogrib Language and Its Family[1]:

The Dogrib language belongs to a close family of about thirty languages. In this Na-Dene or Athapaskan family of languages, Slave and Chipewyan are the most similar to Dogrib. Because of the similarities among the languages, some Dogrib people can understand Slave or Chipewyan.

Languages related to Dogrib are spoken in the western Northwest Territories, northern parts of Manitoba, Saskatchewan, Alberta, and British Columbia, the Yukon Territory, and Alaska. More Na-Dene languages are or were spoken in western parts of Washington, Oregon, and California. In the dry desert plateaus of Colorado, New Mexico, and Arizona, and in some areas of northern Mexican, the southern relatives of the Dogrib language, Apache and Navajo, are spoken.

All of the people who originally spoke Na-Dene languages come from one people, and the Na-Dene languages were once one language. As time passed, and people moved and migrated, the language gradually changed so that people living in different areas now speak their own distinctive Na-Dene languages. The process of change continues today but the shared heritage of the languages means that many words are similar.

Weledeh Dialect:

Just as languages change as they migrate across countries, over time, different regions take on their own dialects because of isolation or exposure to other language groups. While most words remain the same among dialects some pronunciations may shift or change depending on the affecting influence. For example, these stories have been written in the Weledeh dialect of Dogrib. Weledeh is the region closest to Yellowknife and includes the communities of Dettah and Ndilo. Dogrib, in this region, has a strong Chipewyan influence.

[1] The Dogrib Language and Its Family information can be found in Leslie Saxon and Mary Siemens, eds. *Tłįchǫ Yatıì Enįhtł'è*: A Dogrib Dictionary (Dogrib Divisional Board of Education 1992).

Adı łıwe łǫ sıı eyìı tì k'e done netłǫ-lea nàgedè. Xat'ǫ k'e łıwe łǫ gìıchı xè xok'e gha ehgwa łǫ gehtsı̨. Xok'e agòjà hò, ı̨łàà tamı̨ t'à łıwe gìıhchı.

There once was a small group of people who lived on a small fish lake. They had gathered a lot of fish during the fall to make dry fish for the winter. They continued to use their fishnets to catch fish when the winter came.

Xoò tanı ekìyeh łıwe dek'à?į gıìhchı adaade. Xat'ǫ k'e ehgwa hazhǫ gehtsį įlè sìı hazhǫ dàwhìdì adaade. Ts'ehwhįa done gıghǫ nànıgedè adaade, łıwe łǫ gıìchı-le dè, edàanì xoò ghàà egenda ha hǫǫnı gįįwǫ, mbò dęę esagede ha hǫǫnı gįįwǫ.

By the middle of winter, they were catching fewer and fewer fish. They started to eat up all the dry fish they had caught during the fall. Eventually, the people started to worry that they would not catch enough fish for the whole winter and would starve.

Done hazhǫ eɫexè nègįdè t'à ayìı edàgele ha gedı
t'à weghǫ eɫexè gogende. Dǫ įɫè hadı: "Eneèko
įɫè whacho naàde dıı. Įk'ǫ̀ǫ̀ wets'ǫ̀ gedı. Akǫ
wets'ats'ède t'à, asį̀į̀ gots'àdı ha dìı-le wets'èdı t'à
wets'ıı̀ke gedı." Done hazhǫ eneèko ts'ǫ̀ geède.
Łıwe łǫ gıı̀lı-le ajà weghǫ nanègıdè t'à eneèko ts'ǫ̀
hagedı.

The people got together to decide what to do. Someone said:
"There is an old man who lives by himself. He has medicine
power. Let's go and see what he can do." So that is what they
did. The people went over to see the old man. They told him
they were worried about not catching a lot of fish.

Eneèko goòhkw'ǫ. Eyìıtł'ahǫ dıı hagòhdı, "Seʔı̨k'ǫ̀ǫ̀ t'à nàxìts'ahdı k'èxa, segha eye aahtsı̨ gohdì. Nàmbe ı̨k'ǫ̀ǫ̀ sets'ǫ neèt'à, edàanìghǫ łıwe łǫ ààhlì-le wek'aatah ha," gohdì.

The old man listened to them. Afterwards, he told them, "As a gift for my power, make me a drum. I have otter medicine and I will use my otter medicine to see why you are not catching many fish anymore."

Done eye gehtsį weghǫ nagįįt'e hò, eneèko wemǫǫ̀ nègįdè.

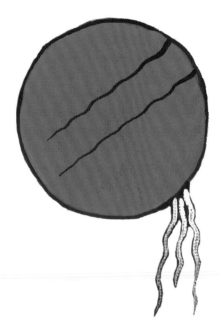

When the people were finished making the drum, they gathered around the old man.

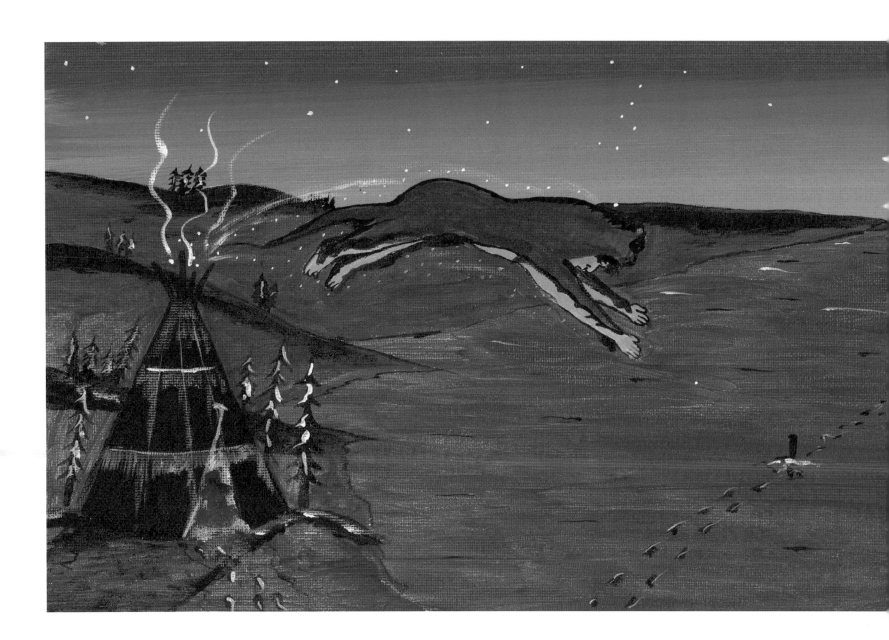

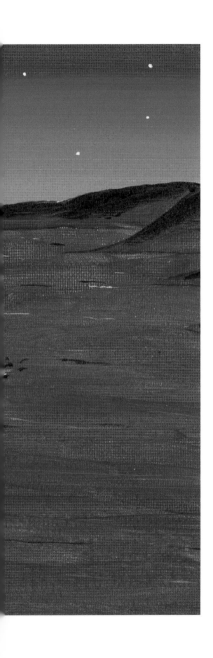

Eneèko weʔɪk'ǫ̀ǫ̀ shɪ t'à ejɪ. Ejɪ nɪet'ìì, weʔɪk'ǫ̀ǫ̀ nàmbe whelɪ xè tèe ts'ǫ̀ tehko, asɪ̀ɪ̀ łɪwe gohłɪ nìì gha tèe k'embe. Nàmbe łɪwe wɪ̱ɪ̱zì gòhʔǫ-le. Nàmbe tɪ welǫ ts'ǫ̀ tèe k'eet'ɪ̱, haanìkò łɪwe wɪ̱ɪ̱zì yaʔɪ̱-le.

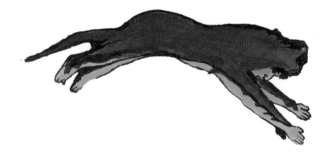

The old man started singing his medicine song. While he was singing, his spirit transformed into an otter and this otter went into the lake, swimming around to look for fish. The otter did not find any fish at all. The otter decided to go to the far end of the lake, but he could not find any fish there either.

Nàmbe tambàa ts'ǫ̀ naìmį eyıts'ǫ eneèko nawhelį t'à eneèko ejıį-le ajà.

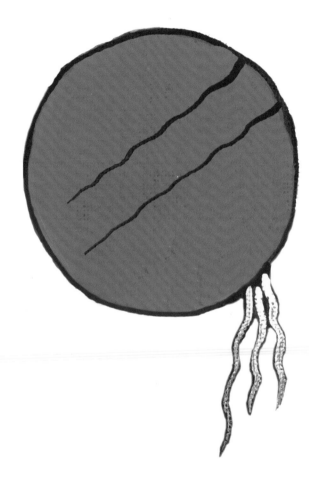

The otter swam back to the shore and entered into the body of the old man and the old man stopped singing.

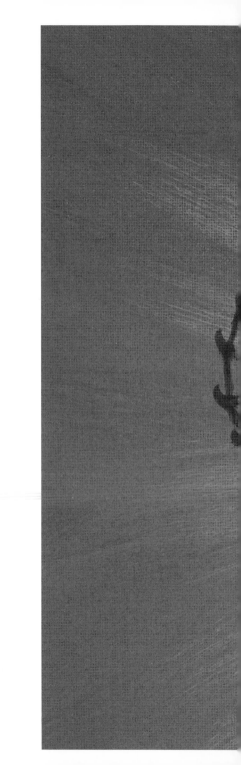

Done hazhǫ wemǫ̀ǫ̀ geèhkw'ee sìɪ dageehke, "Asɪ̀ɪ̀,
łɪwe wenèèʔɪ̨?" Eneèko done ghaı̨da t'à dɪɪ hadɪ,
"Įlè, łɪwe wɪ̨ɪ̨zì eehʔɪ̨-le dìì." Done gɪgha dìì agòjà.

The people around him started asking him questions; "Well,
did you see any fish?" The old man looked at them and said,
"No, I saw no fish in the lake." The people were desperate.

Achį įdàedzę̀ę̀ nındè wį̀įdza nǫ̀ǫ̀ gehdì.

They asked the old man to try again the next day.

Įdàedzę̀ę̀ done hazhǫ achį eneèko wemǫ̀ǫ̀ nègįdè.
Eneèko weʔįk'ǫ̀ǫ̀ shį t'à ejį. Achį nàmbe whelį.

The next day the people gathered around the old man again.

The old man started to sing his medicine song. His spirit left

his body and again became an otter.

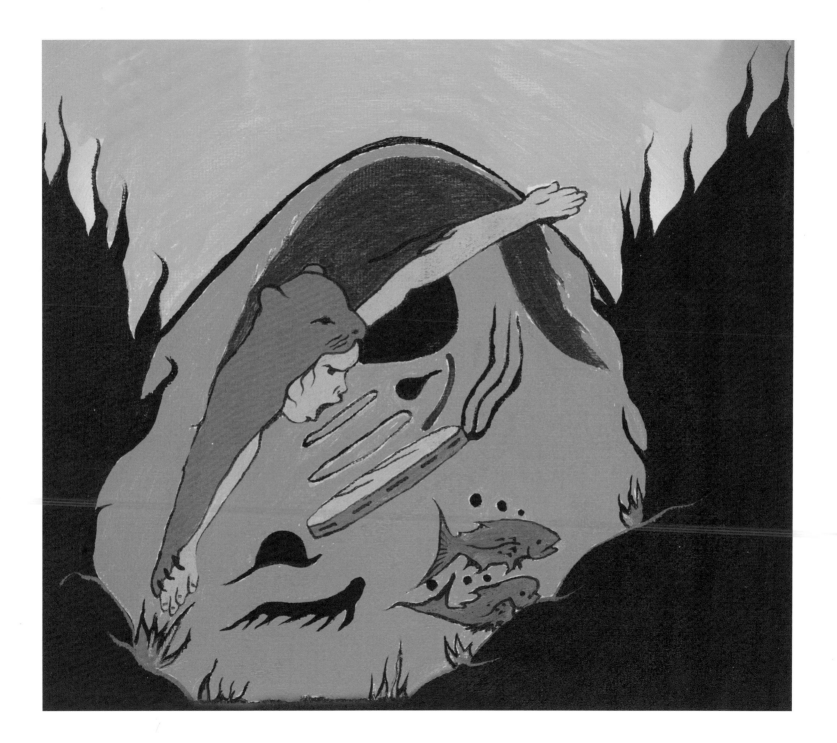

Dıı t'à nàmbe tèe denahk'e tagǫįhwhà k'aʔehta ha nıwǫ. Akǫ nìtła hò, wetł'ahk'eh nǫ̀, akǫ wets'ǫ̀ gǫ̀ʔà, ndè goyìı gǫ̀ʔà nechàa wègaat'į. Akǫ goyaàgǫ̀ʔà gà įhdaa nàke tįdà hogıìhdı nǫ̀.

This time the otter decided to go deep into the deepest part of the lake. There, to the otter's surprise, was a huge hole with two large jackfish guarding the entrance.

Nàmbe akǫ goyìı ts'ǫ̀ k'eet'į̀ hò, goyìı edlatłǫ lemì łıwe gohłį̀ yaàʔį.

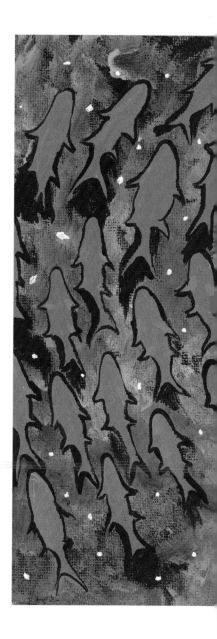

The otter saw that inside the hole there were thousands and thousands of fish.

Nàmbe įhdaa łak'aà łaįhdè t'à, łıwe hazhǫ hàède agǫįlà. Nàmbe sìı yıghǫ xahòdì. Įwhąt'ı nàmbe done nawhelį.

The otter killed the two jackfish that were keeping all of the fish. He freed the fish from the hole. The otter was really excited. Quickly, he returned back into the old man.

Eneèko hadı, "Naxìmı̀ k'aahta! Naxìmı̀ k'aahta!"
Done hazhǫ gıı̀nà agòjà. Tǫ k'e mı̀ k'agehta ha ts'ǫ̀
geède.

The old man said, "Check your nets! Check your nets!"
Everyone was excited. They all went onto the ice to check
their nets.

Łıwe ghǫ tamì dàgoòʔǫ t'à ahjǫ tǫ nahyı̨ nee!

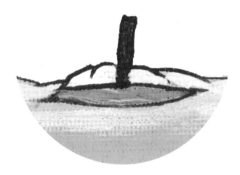

They found them full of fish, so full that the nets were melting a hole in the ice!

Done hazhǫ sìɪ gɪnà. Eyìɪ toòt'ìɪ eneèko nàmbe weʔɨk'ǫ̀ wets'ǫ̀ gha nàhsɨ nechàa hò hoòlɨ.

The people were all so happy. Later that night there was a huge feast in honour of the old man who had the otter medicine.

The End.

Hòt'a Welǫ.

Dogrib Orthography and Pronunciations

Dene Font:

The Dogrib language is written using the Dene font. You will notice that the letter "ɪ" is not dotted in this font. This is to avoid confusion with the low tone markings used in the Dogrib language "ì".

Dogrib Alphabet:

There are forty-one letters in the Dogrib alphabet. It has four "plain vowels" (a e i o) which can change through nasal and tonal markings, resulting in sixteen different ways to express vowel sounds:

Plain Vowels - the air, which makes the sound of these vowels, flows through the mouth like vowels in English, e.g., **i** as in **di,** this sounds like the i in the word sk<u>i</u>.

Nasal Vowels - the air flows through the nose and the mouth, e.g., ɪ as in **dɪ** sounds like the e in the word m<u>e</u>an.

Low Tone Plain Vowels - the air flows through the mouth, and the tone is held a little bit longer with a low voice e.g., **ìè** as in **dìè** sounds like dee in English but it is held longer.

Low Tone Nasal Vowels - the air flows through the nose and the mouth, and the tone is held a little bit longer with a low voice e.g., **ɪ̀** as in **dɪ̀ɪ̀** (four times), sounds like "mean" but the vowel sound is held a little longer.

The following chart lists all of the Dogrib letters, and provides Dogrib words that illustrate the sound of the letters and shows the closest English equivalent to the Dogrib sound.

You can listen to the sounds of the above vowels, letters and words on your computer with the attached multimedia CD or if you do not have a computer you can place the CD into your CD player to follow along.

Letter	Dogrib Word	English Translation	Closest English Sound
ʔ	ʔah tł'àʔeh	snowshoe pants	the 'click' sound which we hear in the expression "oh-oh"
a	amà ladà	mother table	<u>fa</u>ther; when **a** is nasalized (ą), it is similar to the sound in w<u>an</u>t
b	bebì k'ehbe	baby I am swimming	<u>b</u>a<u>b</u>y
ch	chǫ nechà	rain it is big	<u>ch</u>; some people pronounce this sound more like what we hear in we<u>ts</u>uit
ch'	ch'oh sech'à	quill against me	the same as **ch**, but with the 'click' sound as part of it
d	done nedè	person your younger sister	<u>d</u>i<u>d</u>
dl	dlįa nàʔets'edlò	mouse we are laughing	ba<u>dl</u>y; or sometimes like <u>gl</u>ue
dz	dzèh edza	spruce gum cold weather	a<u>dz</u>e
e	ehtł'è wetà hęʔę	mud, dirt his or her father yes	s<u>e</u>t; when **e** is nasalized, it is similar to the sound in s<u>en</u>t; in a prefix after **w**, it is similar to w<u>oo</u>d
g	gah nàhgą gomǫ	rabbit bushman our mother	<u>g</u>o
gh	segha weghàts'eeda	for me we are looking at it	no similar sound in English; similar to the <u>r</u> sound in the French *rouge* "red"
gw	ehgwàa	dryfish	lan<u>gu</u>age
h	hanì ehtsèe	in this way grandfather	<u>h</u>at; in Dogrib this sound can be pronounced inside or at the end of a word
ı	lıdì mį̀ yeht'ì	tea fish net she or he is pulling it	sk<u>i</u>; when **i** is nasalized, it is similar to the sound in m<u>ea</u>ns

j	**j**ıe **j**ǫ de**j**ı̨	berry here she or he is scared	jet; some people pronounce this sound more like what we hear in a<u>dz</u>e
k	**k**e ts'è**k**o	footwear woman	<u>k</u>it; in prefixes, it is sometimes pronounced like **x** or **h**
k'	**k'**àle e**k'**ı̨̀	spider fish eggs	the same as **k**, but with the "click" sound as part of it
kw	**kw**e e**kw**ǫ̀	rock caribou	<u>qu</u>it
kw'	**kw'**ah e**kw'**ǫ̀ǫ̀	moss bones	the same as **kw**, but with the "click" sound as part of it
l	**l**ıdì e**l**à	tea canoe	<u>l</u>et
ł	**ł**ǫ e**ł**exè	many together	breathy <u>l</u>; similar to the <u>l</u> in fli<u>p</u> or s<u>l</u>ip
m	**m**ı̀ **m**asì	fish net thank you	<u>m</u>et
mb	ı̨**mb**è **mb**ò **mb**eh	summer meat knife	ru<u>mb</u>le; many people use the **b** sound instead of **mb**
n	**n**ezı̨ go**n**è	it is good our land	<u>n</u>et; sometimes **n** is contracted with a vowel to make a nasalized vowel
nd	sı̨**nd**e **nd**ı	my older brother island	sa<u>nd</u>al; many people use the **d** sound instead of **nd**
o	ł**o** det'**o**ch**o** whek'**ò**	smoke eagle it is cold	g<u>o</u>; some people pronounce this sound more like g<u>oo</u>; when **o** is nasalized, it is similar to the sound in d<u>o</u>n't
r	ʔo**r**ı	spruce bough	similar to ca<u>rr</u>y; some people almost never use this sound and just leave it out
s	**s**a **s**echıa	month, sun my little brother	<u>s</u>et
sh	**sh**ı̀h deh**sh**e	mountain it is growing	<u>sh</u>ort; some people pronounce this sound more like what we we hear in <u>s</u>ort

t	**t**ı ne**t**à	water your father	<u>t</u>en
t'	**t'**eeko **t'**asah**t'**e-le	young woman I'm fine	the same as **t**, but with the "click" sound as part of it
tł	**tł**ı̨ dane**tł**o	dog dance!	se<u>tt</u>le; or sometimes more like <u>cl</u>ue
tł'	**tł'**ı enı̨h**tł'**è	rope paper, book	the same as **tł**, but with the "click" sound as part of it
ts	**ts**o eh**ts**ı̨	firewood granny	ca<u>ts</u>
ts'	**ts'**ah **ts'**ǫ̀ko	hat old woman	the same as **ts**, but with the "click" sound as part of it
w	**w**età lıdì**w**ò	his or her father teabag	<u>w</u>et; in a prefix, **w** with a following **e** sounds similar to <u>woo</u>d
wh	**wh**a lıdì deh**wh**ǫ	marten I want tea	breathy <u>wh</u> as in <u>wh</u>en; in a prefix, **wh** with a following **e** sounds like <u>whi</u>rr.
x	**x**ah go**x**è **x**ok'e	goose with us winter	no similar sound in English; a raspy h, similar to the German <u>ch</u> as in *Bach* (the composer)
y	**y**ahtı k'e**y**ege kw'à**y**ı̨̀ą	priest carrying bowl	<u>y</u>et
z	**z**ǫ de**z**ǫ lı**z**à whe**z**ò	only it is black ace (in cards) it is crooked	<u>z</u>oo
zh	**zh**aka goı̨h**zh**ı̨ı̨ goı**zh**ǫ ı**zh**ìı	the top of the snow shadows he or she is smart down	plea<u>s</u>ure; some people pronounce this sound more like what we hear in plea<u>se</u>

Source: Leslie Saxon and Mary Siemens, eds. *Tłı̨chǫ Yatıì Enı̨htł'è: A Dogrib Dictionary* (Dogrib Divisional Board of Education 1992).

John Blondin (March 6, 1960 – April 27, 1996)

The late John Blondin is the son of George Blondin, a well-known and respected Dene Elder. He was a talented dancer, graphic artist, and founder of a local Native theatre group. John worked through a museum education outreach program at the Prince of Wales Northern Heritage Centre where John celebrated the Dene culture by performing the stories he had learned from his father. This story, *The Old Man with the Otter Medicine,* was one of John's favourite stories.

Photo Courtesy of Prince of Wales Northern Heritage Centre

George Blondin

A respected Elder and storyteller, George Blondin maintains the storytelling traditions of the Dene people. He is the author of several books where he depicts the tales of medicine heroes, hunters and healers who have forged Dene history. George currently resides in Behchoko, NWT where he continues to share and write the stories of the Dene people.

Archie Beaverho, Illustrator

Archie Beaverho was born in Wha Ti in 1965. He is an accomplished painter and cartoonist whose understanding of his culture is reflected in his work. Archie still lives in Wha Ti and currently works at Diavik Mines.

Mary Rose Sundberg, Translator and Dogrib Narration

Mary Rose is a true advocate for her language and people. As translator, interpreter, teacher and community member, Mary Rose works tirelessly to promote the teaching and revitalization of the Dogrib language. She founded Goyatiko, a small language centre in Dettah NWT where she produces language materials and teaches language classes.

Photo Courtesy of Barb Cameron